The Village

Bluebell Wood

Buttercup
Cottage

Hardwick House

River
Noodle

SIMON & SCHUSTER BOOKS FOR YOUNG READERS
An imprint of Simon & Schuster Children's Publishing Division
1230 Avenue of the Americas, New York, New York 10020
Text copyright © 2009 by Sarah Ferguson, The Duchess of York
Illustrations copyright © 2009 by Sam Williams
Published simultaneously in Great Britain by Simon & Schuster UK as *Little Red to the Rescue*
All rights reserved, including the right of reproduction in whole or in part in any form.
SIMON & SCHUSTER BOOKS FOR YOUNG READERS is a trademark of Simon & Schuster, Inc.
LITTLE RED is a trademark of Sarah Ferguson, The Duchess of York, and is used under license.
Book design by David Bennett
The text for this book is set in Goudy.
The illustrations for this book are rendered in soft pencil and watercolor on Arches paper.
Manufactured in China
2 4 6 8 10 9 7 5 3
Library of Congress Cataloging-in-Publication Data
York, Sarah Mountbatten-Windsor, Duchess of, 1959–
Little Red's autumn adventure / Sarah Ferguson, The Duchess of York ;
illustrated by Sam Williams. — 1st ed.
p. cm.
Summary: On her way to the Great Harvest Festival in Bluebell Wood,
Little Red's bag of magic dust falls into the wrong paws when she tries to help two lost mice.
ISBN: 978-0-689-84341-9 (hardcover)
[1. Dolls—Fiction. 2. Autumn—Fiction. 3. Magic—Fiction. 4. Friendship—Fiction.] I. Williams, Sam, 1955- ill. II. Title.
PZ7.Y823Lg 2009
[E]—dc22
2008042625

Little Red's
Autumn Adventure

Sarah Ferguson
The Duchess of York

Illustrated by
Sam Williams

SIMON & SCHUSTER BOOKS FOR YOUNG READERS
New York   London   Toronto   Sydney

It was a splendid autumn afternoon at Buttercup Cottage. Little Red and her friends were on their way to the Great Harvest Festival in Bluebell Wood. They kicked up the golden leaves as they went along, humming a jolly tune. "What a whizz of a windy day!" cried Little Blue excitedly.

A giant oak leaf floated down past them.
Gino jumped to catch it.

"I know!" said Little Red,
clapping her hands. "Let's do
a bit of leaf-boarding!"

Everyone rushed to gather up the biggest leaves they could find and then scampered to the top of the hill.

"Wait for me!" called Roany as the others all went zooming past. "I'll never find a leaf that's my size," she sniffed.

Little Red jumped off her leaf-board. "Don't worry, dear old Roany," she said as she reached for her sack of smiles.

Then, with a teeny sprinkling of magic dust, she turned a tiny leaf into a Roany-size leaf-board.

Off Roany sped with a happy *neigh-h-h*, and Little Red dashed off to catch up with the others.

Wheee!

Suddenly, Little Red's leaf hit a rather large tuft of grass . . .

BUMPITY-BUMP, BUMPITY . . . WHOOPS!

. . . and she went tumbly-tumble, head-over-heels,
and landed at the foot of a big blackberry bush.

"Whoopsee!" Little Red laughed as she untangled herself.

Just then, she heard the teeniest of *squeak-squeaks* coming from under the blackberries. "Mommy?" said a very small voice.

Little Red knelt down to have a look. Peering out from the shadows of the leaves, two tiny mice clung to each other.

"Eek!" they squeaked, jumping back and gripping each other all the more tightly.

"Don't worry," said Little Red in her sweetest, kindest voice. "I'll help you!"

"But you're so BIG!" peeped one tiny mouse. "And SCARY!" whispered the other.

So Little Red reached into her sack of smiles, grabbed a
handful of magic dust, sprinkled it over her head, and . . .

ZIPPITY DOO DAH!

she shrunk right down to the size of the tiny mice!

"There, that's better," she
said. "Now, tell me, what
ever is the matter?"

"We can't find our mommy!" squeaked the tiny mice. "We were on our way to the harvest festival and we were playing hide-and-seek with the butterflies, but then they flew away and we were lost!"

"I'm sure your mommy isn't far," said Little Red.
"Come on, we'll find her together." But when Little Red
reached down for her sack of smiles, it was gone!

Then she remembered. There, high above their heads, the sack of smiles hung from the brambles. "Oh, snaggaroo!" she said to herself. "However will I find Mommy Mouse now? And how will I reach my sack of smiles?"

Little Red smiled her bravest smile. "Don't worry, little ones, follow me." And she whistled a merry song as they set off on the long journey to the harvest festival.

Meanwhile, Little Blue, Gino, and Roany had arrived at the clearing where the festival was nearly ready to begin. It was quite a sight indeed! Here, there, and everywhere, the animals were frantically making the final preparations.

Blakesley Bill was directing the robins as they strung lanterns from the trees. Purdey was scurrying to and fro, setting up the band. There were towering tables, brimming with all sorts of tasty treats. Roany licked her lips. "Wait till Little Red sees this!" But when they looked around, Little Red was nowhere to be seen.

Just then, Mrs. Mouse came rushing up to Roany,
wringing her apron in distress. "Oh, deary me!" she cried.
"I've lost two of my children. They're always running off,
and I had my hands full with the plum pie . . . Oh, please,
can you help me?"

Little Blue looked at Roany. Roany looked at Little Blue.
Little Red would know what to do—but where on earth was
she? The sun was setting, and long purple shadows were already
stretching across the grass. They were very worried indeed.

"I think . . . ," said Roany, "I think we should make a
search party."

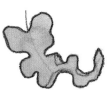

The friends hadn't been searching for long when . . .

THUNK!

An acorn landed squarely in the middle
of Little Blue's bumblebee bobble hat!

"Ouch!" said Little Blue, and he looked
up. "Purdey," he said slowly, "what color do
the leaves turn in the autumn?"

"Why, you know that, Little Blue. They
turn red, and gold, and orange . . ."

Everyone looked up to where Little Blue
was pointing, his mouth wide open in
astonishment!

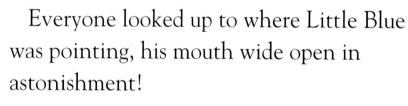

Up above, the leaves on the trees had turned every splendiferous color in the rainbow! There were pink leaves and blue leaves, spotty leaves and stripy leaves. The friends couldn't believe their eyes!

Then Little Blue spied someone, a very mischievous someone, high in the branches. Gripped tightly in his paws was . . .

. . . Little Red's sack of smiles. The magic dust was spilling here, there, and everywhere, mixing up the colors of the leaves!

"You naughty squirrel!" cried Little Blue. "Come back down and give us back the sack of smiles!" But the squirrel just chattered and tittered and scurried even farther up a tree trunk.

Realizing that something needed to be done—and fast—Little Blue bent down and pinched a bit of the magic dust between his fingers. Then, reaching his arm up over his head, he sprinkled the dust onto his bumblebee bobble hat, saying, "Buzzy bee, carry me!"

All at once, the bumblebee bobble started to spin and buzz, and before the friends knew it, Little Blue was lifted off the ground. Up, up, up he flew, right to the tops of the trees, until he was eye-to-eye with the naughty squirrel.

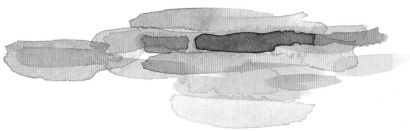

In a flash, Little Blue
snatched back the sack of smiles.
"This belongs to Little Red! Where did you
find it?" Little Blue demanded to know.
"Why, just down there!" giggled the
squirrel, pointing toward a blackberry bush.

Little Blue sounded the alarm on his trumpet and yelled,
"Little Red, Little Red, can you hear me?"

Down below, Little Red heard the trumpet and Little Blue's cry. "Now, tiny mice," she said, "I need you to shout out as loud as you can!

"Okay, on the count of three—one, two, three . . ." "Here, Little Blue!" they all cried. "We're over here, by the spotty toadstool!"

From the top of his tree, Little Blue heard the faint squeaks of the three lost friends and, without wasting a second, he *buzz-buzz-buzz*ed down to the spot where they were sheltering.

"Oh, well done, Little Blue, you've found us!" said Little Red. "Now, sprinkle me with the tiniest bit of magic dust!" So Little Blue closed his eyes, reached into the sack of smiles, and . . .

ZA-ZING!

Little Red sprang back up to her jolly old self.

"Oh, thank heavens!" Little Red laughed and gave Little Blue an enormous hug. Everyone was overjoyed—most of all Mrs. Mouse and her nine tiny mice!

And when, at last, the friends finally reached the festival, they had a wonderful time, dancing and singing under the great harvest moon, long into the night.

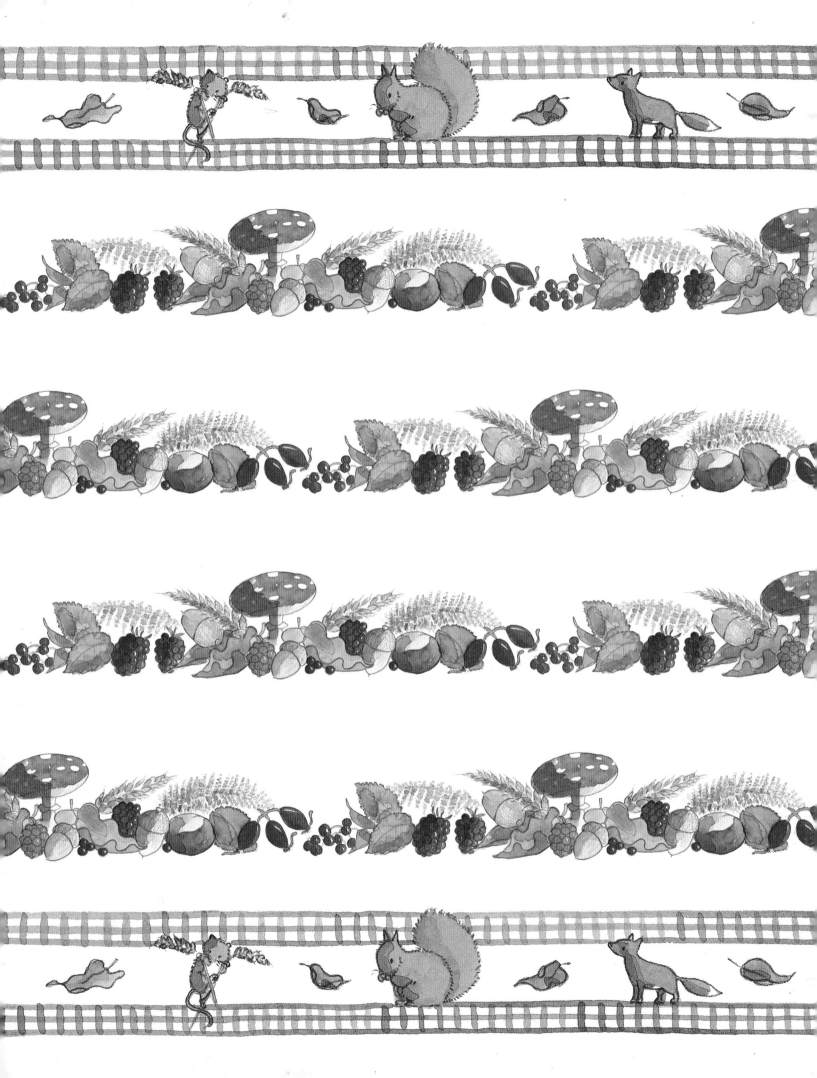